I0712682

EGYPT
IN
TIME?
Story by
Ness Uskert
Pictures by
Michael Bryan Quiambao

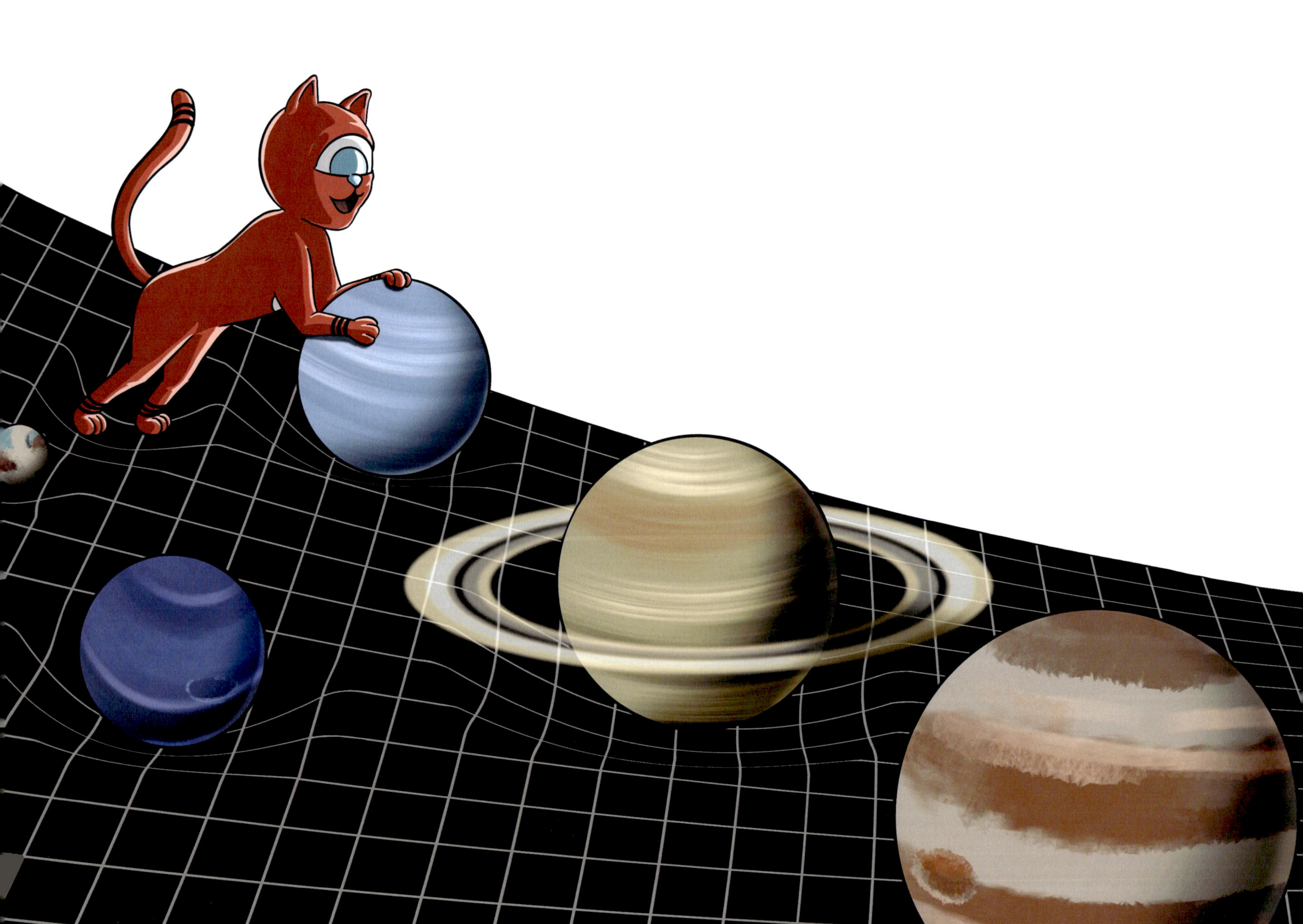

Thank you, Grandma, for supporting my passions, even if they stretch as far as "sewing" the fabric of time!

One afternoon, Egypt finds Ness in his workshop tinkering with a strange device.

E = mc²

Si Li I Be
Spaces and Dimensions
TIME

Mesmerized,
Egypt reaches
out and
touches it with
his paw.

of Elements
TIME
As if by magic, Ness and Egypt get sucked into the donut-like device.

Md
Ra
Dy
Au
Rn

Egypt and Ness fall for what feels like a very long time.

MISCELLANEOUS

Suddenly, their endless fall ends.

Before they are able to process their surroundings, the device opens another portal and Ness and Egypt are transported in time again.

This happens over and over again
as they jump from century to
century, spanning history.

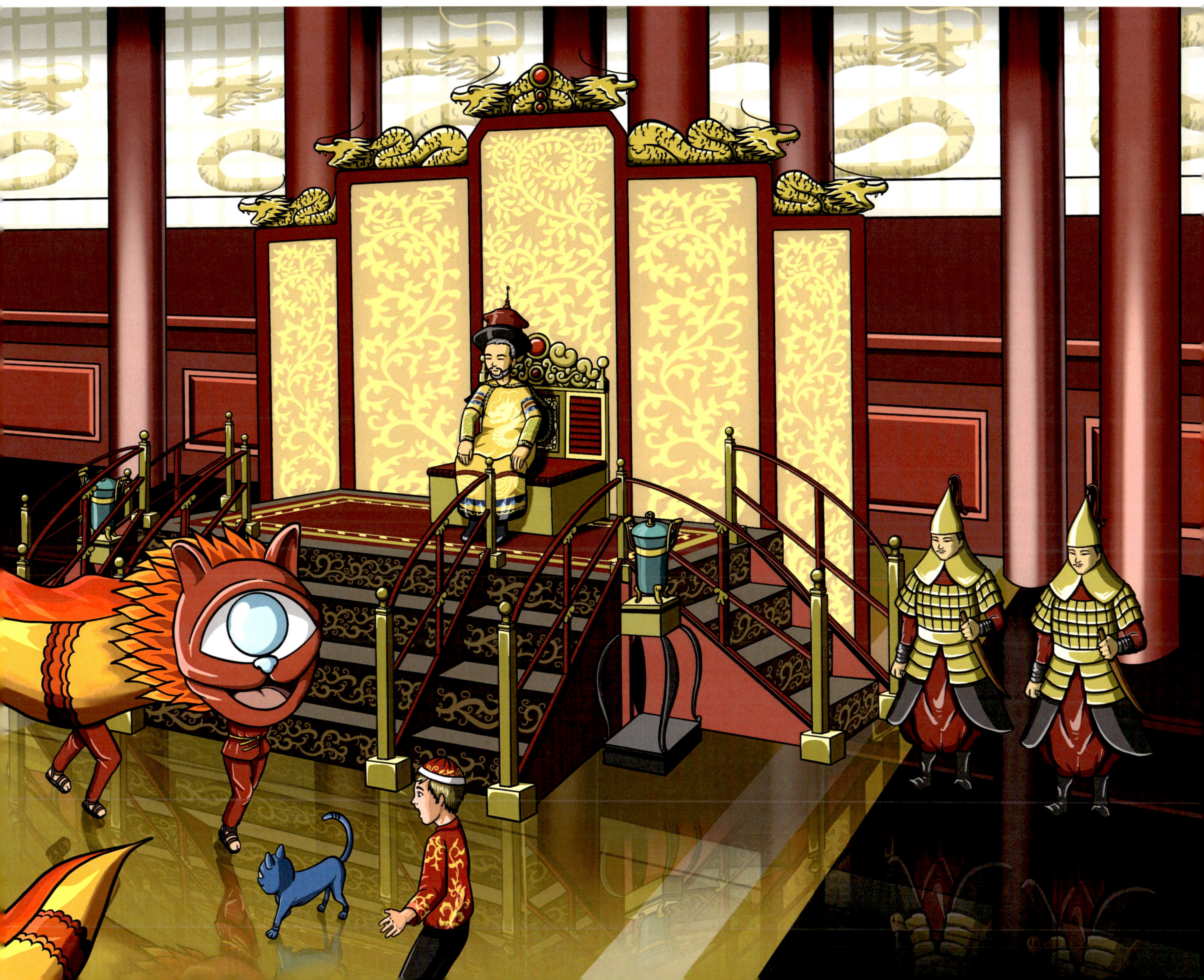

As they start to become seasoned time travelers, they embrace their situation…

...and start having adventures!

They learn about other cultures and places.

They even begin to fight for causes that they feel are just.

But when their time machine is hit by a spear, they feel themselves pulled away once again.

Except this time, they find themselves not in the past, but in the future!

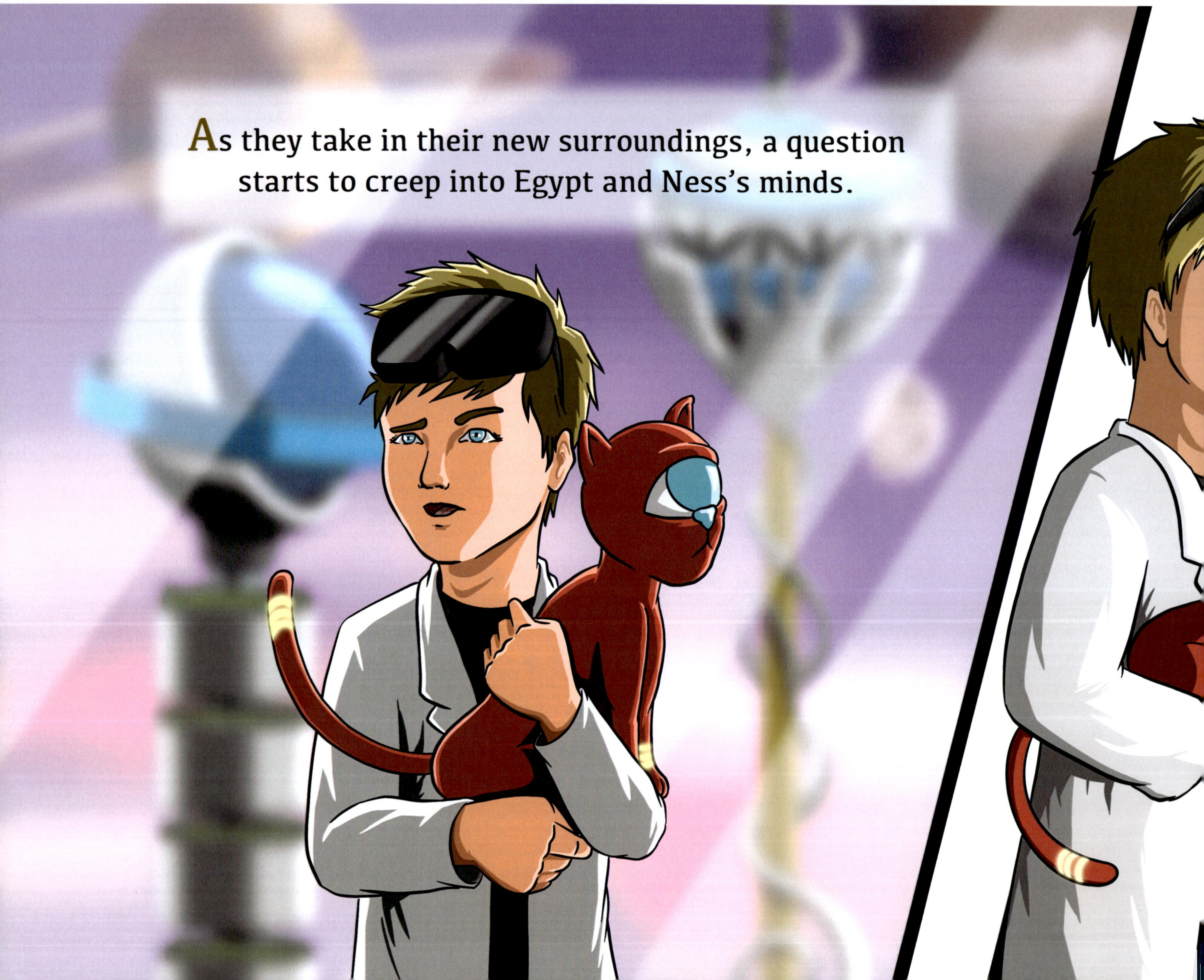
As they take in their new surroundings, a question starts to creep into Egypt and Ness's minds.

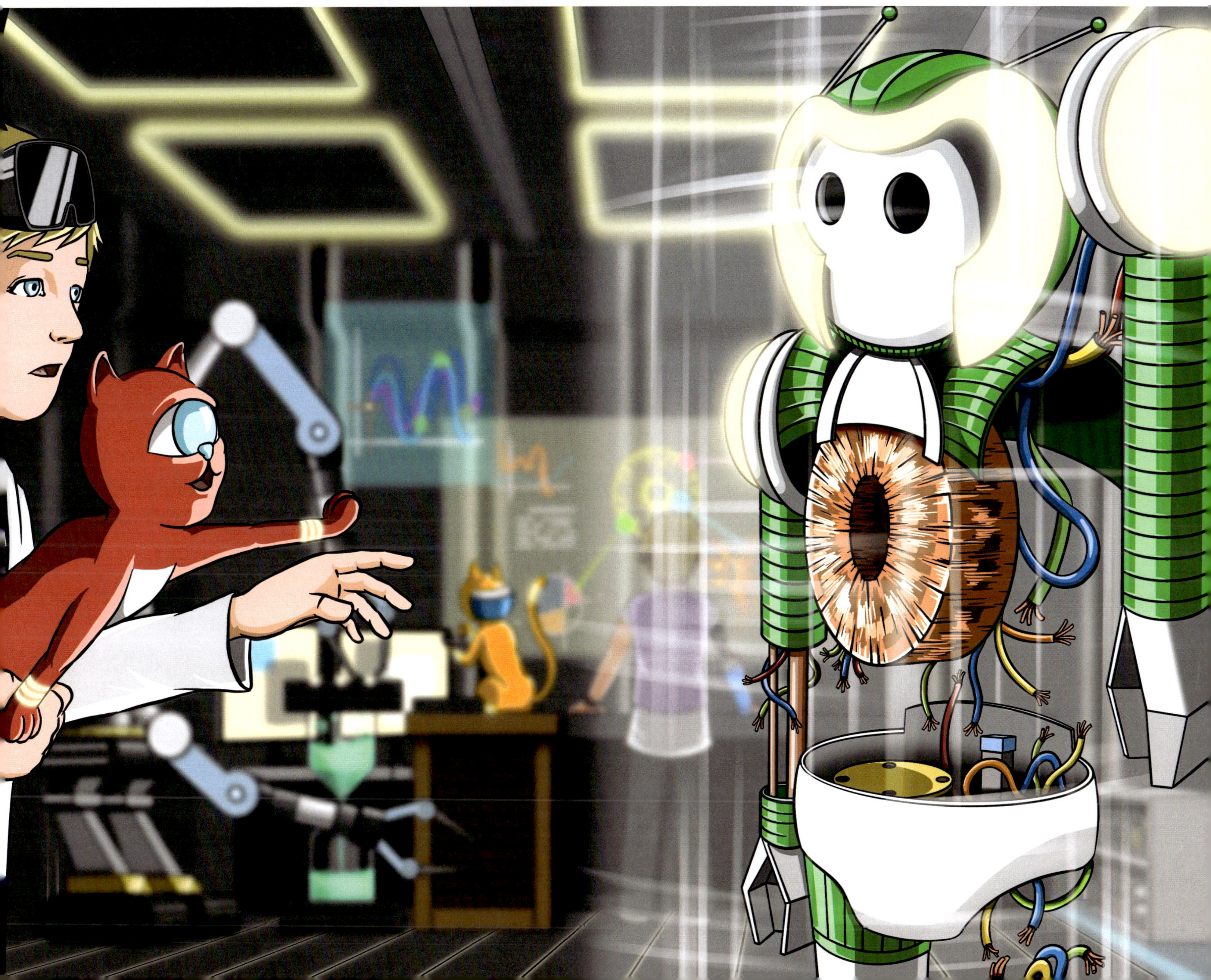

How are we going to get home?

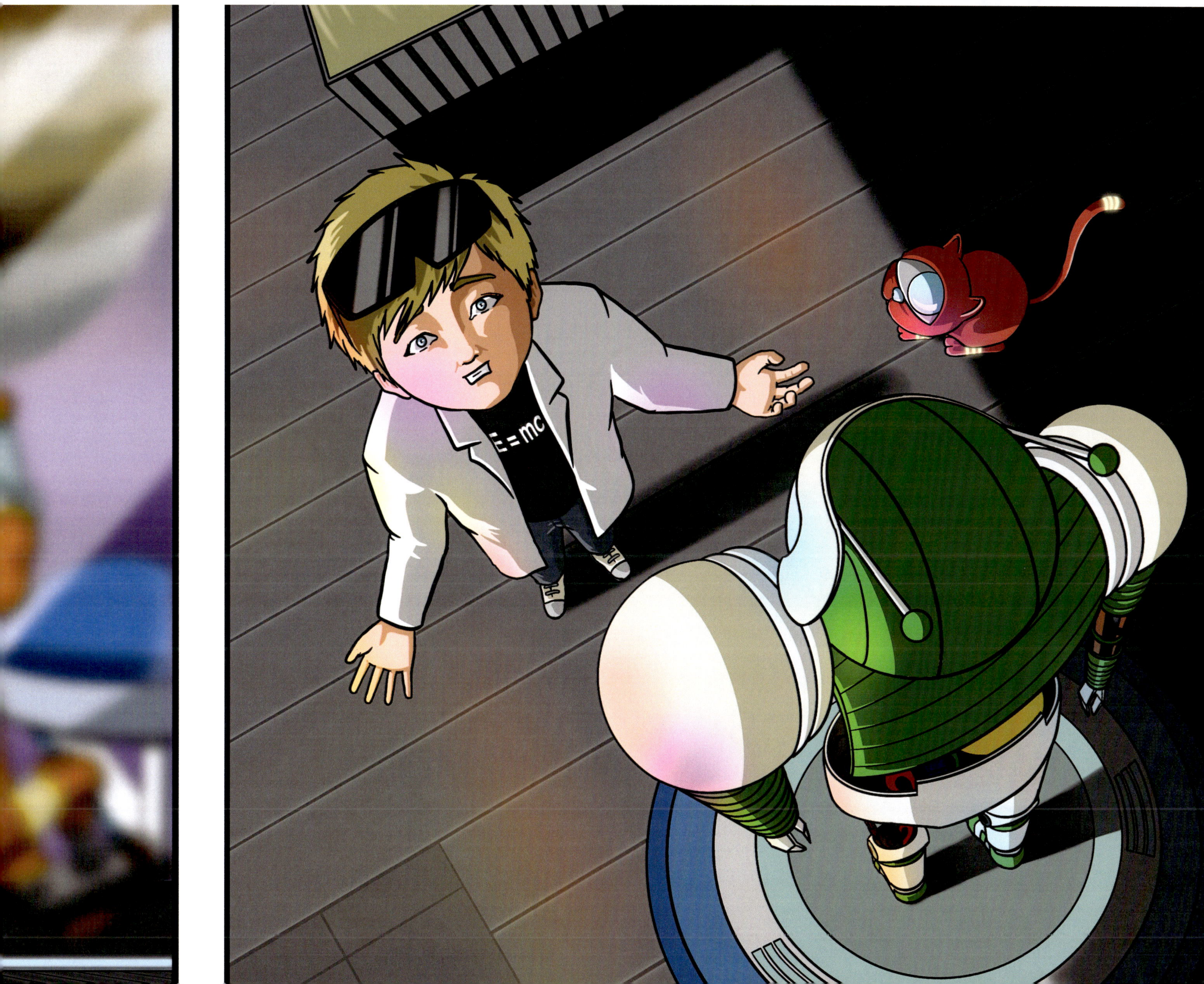

They explore and search for clues.

E=mc

Suddenly, Egypt encounters a strange creature that brings him to someone who can help.

Egypt finds Ness and introduces
his new friend.

It's me!
In the future!

After listening to their story,
Future Ness agrees to send
them home.

Future Ness shows them his time travel creation.
But be warned! When you get home there may be some surprises.

Ooh!
Aah!

This time they fall through
time with a smile.

Ness and Egypt are back home.
Uh-oh, Egypt, I think Future Ness was right! It looks like home, but something is different!

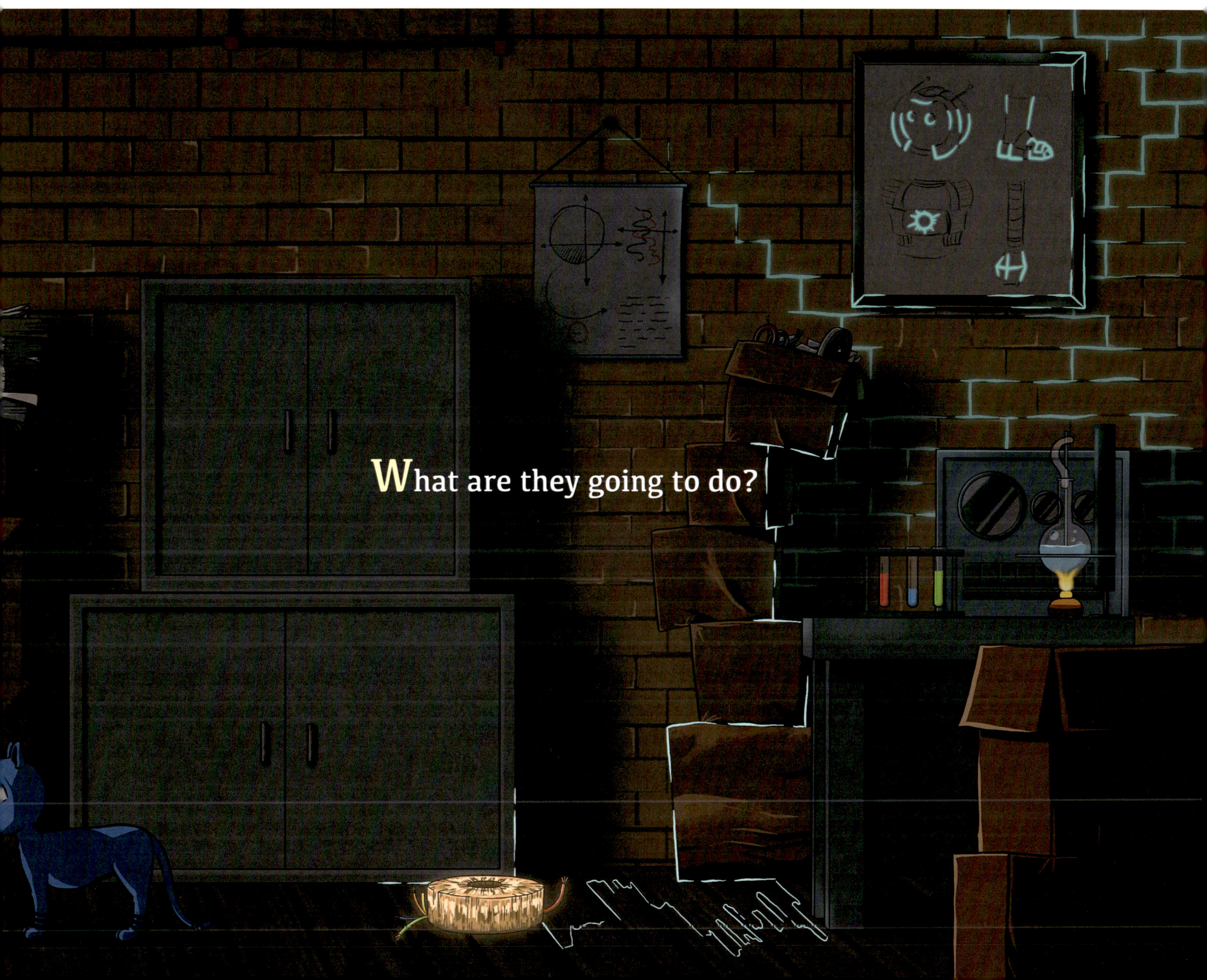
What are they going to do?

WWW.EGYPTTHECAT.COM